*To Umar, Mahir, Noor, and my mother.*

With special thanks to Jamal J. Elias
and Sameera Raja
for their advice and support.

Each morning during *Ramadan*, also known as *Ramzan*, Raza woke to the sound of a siren. The dull but steady sound announced sunrise, the time when Muslims who intend to fast stopped eating or drinking till sunset. Since he was eight years old, Raza did not fast. The elders were served *Sehri*, or the pre-dawn breakfast first, and then came the turn of the children.

Raza loved eating Sehri on weekends when he was allowed to get up that early. The special breakfast, served while the stars still roamed the sky, typically consisted of hot, flaky parathas, spicy eggs, a yogurt drink called *lassi*, and mugs of steaming chai tea.

One weekday night he was awakened by an unusual sound.

# The Jinni on the Roof

## A Ramadan Story

Written by Natasha Rafi

Illustrated by Abdul Malik Channa

ISBN: 0988864908
ISBN 13: 9780988864900
Library of Congress Control Number: 2013908657
Pamir LLC Clinton Corners, NY

"Is that the siren or the *Azan?*" he wondered. The Azan was the call to prayer, which followed the siren. But as he rubbed his eyes and strained to listen, he realized it was pitch dark outside. Then he heard the sound again—khurrrrrrrrrrrr, spheeeeeee. Now he knew what it was.

"Oh, that's Uncle Hasan snoring," he said to himself. For several minutes Raza listened to the train-like whistle that seemed to leave his uncle's mouth as he breathed out. Then another sound distracted him.

"Wait a minute, what's that?" Thump, thud, thump. "That sounds like Amina." Amina the cook was heaving her plump, doughy body up the stairs to his grandmother's room to wake her up. She had a lot of work to do since the whole family had gathered together in Lahore to celebrate *Eid-ul-Fitr,* the holiday that marks the end of Ramadan.

Shortly after that came the aroma.

Aaah, the delicious smell of *parathas* as they crackled and sizzled in the hot oil!

Raza's mouth started to water. "I can't wait till the children's breakfast," he thought. "I've got to find a way to have Sehri, even though I have school today."

9

Raza stuffed a pillow under his blanket to make it look like he was asleep. Then he crept out of his room. Very quietly he made his way through his grandmother's rambling home. The house was filled with cousins, aunts, and uncles.

"I've got to get to the roof without getting caught," he muttered to himself. On his way he passed through room after room filled with heavy wood furniture, stubbing his toe in the dark more than once. Luckily, the well-worn carpets hushed the sounds of his steps. Finally, he reached the stairs to the roof.

Once on the roof, Raza made his way to the chimney that was directly over the kitchen. As he leaned in and listened, he could hear the muffled sound of Amina humming as she worked.

"She is probably laying out the balls of dough in neat rows for the parathas," he thought. Raza took a deep breath, tried to make his voice sound as deep as possible, and bellowed into the chimney.

"Amina!" he called, and then again, "Amina!"

Poor Amina. The sound of his voice through the tunnel of the chimney was creepy indeed. She dropped her rolling pin onto her foot and yelped in pain. Hearing her cry encouraged Raza, and he bellowed, "Amina, I want you to make some parathas for me!"

Once she heard that, Amina rushed out of the kitchen and ran toward Raza's grandmother's room. "Help, help!" she stammered. "There is a *jinni* in the house." A jinni was a mysterious creature, and Amina had told Raza many stories about them. Seeing Amina's state, Raza's grandmother was quite alarmed. Amina was pale, sweating and trembling.

"A jinni?" she asked. "Where?"

"In the kitchen," said Amina, in a wobbly voice.

"What does he want?" said Raza's grandmother, wondering if Amina had awakened from a bad dream that night.

"He wants parathas," she replied.

"Parathas?"

"Yes, parathas," said Amina. "That's what he said."

"I will come with you to the kitchen," said Raza's grandmother.

They made their way to the kitchen, and Amina called out, "Is anyone there?"

It was cold and dark on the roof. When he finally heard her voice again, Raza leaned over once more and said in the deepest voice he could manage, "Amina, make me parathas, and leave them on the roof with a blanket. Or you shall be sorry."

When she heard that, Raza's grandmother whispered to Amina. "Tell him you will do as he says."

Amina tilted her head toward the roof and said, "The parathas will be ready shortly, sir."

Muttering prayers to herself and blowing out imaginary candles around her in the traditional way of warding off evil, Amina went about cooking a batch of parathas. She wrapped them in a cloth and placed them in a straw basket. Then she went to the linen closet and got out a warm blanket.

"Who would have thought jinn need blankets?" she wondered.

While Amina was busy with her chores, Raza's grandmother went to the children's bedroom, and looked around. After that she went back to her room, sat at her desk, and wrote a note.

Then she made her way back to the kitchen where Amina, looking rather nervous, had the basket ready. Raza's grandmother put her note in the basket on top of the parathas and told Amina to take it to the roof.

"Don't worry, everything will be fine," she said.

Reassured, Amina climbed the steps to the roof and carefully opened the door. She took a quick look around but saw no one. She placed the basket and the blanket on an old table and quickly made her way back down the stairs. She was not going to take any chances with a jinni!

When Raza was sure she was gone, he scampered over to the basket. The delectable smell of parathas made its way through the cloth and basket up to his nose, and he chuckled to himself.

"This was so easy," he thought. "Now I can get Amina to make me whatever I want."

When he opened the lid, he saw the note. It was addressed to The Jinni on the Roof.

Confused, Raza opened the letter. It read:

*Dear Jinni,*
*After your breakfast, please come and see your*
*grandmother.*
*Your Nani*

Oh dear! Raza realized he had been caught. Now the parathas didn't seem as tempting as before. Nevertheless, he wolfed them down as he pondered his fate. By then the grown-ups were eating Sehri, and from the peals of laughter coming from the dining room, Raza knew his prank was known to all.

He decided to creep back down and sneak into bed. Maybe he could pretend this never happened. But as soon as he reached the bottom of the stairs, his grandmother appeared.

"Raza," she said. "You know that Ramadan is a holy month when we make a special effort to be extra patient, truthful, and kind. You could not wait for breakfast, deceived Amina, and frightened her. You need to apologize to her, and to make it up to her, you have to help her wash the dishes after every *Iftar,* the evening feast, till the end of Ramadan."

Raza realized his Nani was right. How would he be able to fast in the future if he could not even wait for breakfast? He apologized to Amina, who forgave him and told him many more stories about jinn during his nightly duty. On *Chand Raat,* or the Night of the New Moon, when the elders declared it to be the last fast with the festival of Eid beginning the next day, no one was happier than Raza. He had had enough of dishwashing to last for quite some time!

The following year, Raza kept his first *roza,* or fast. Amina made him extra parathas for breakfast, and his favorite dishes were made for Iftar. To celebrate the occasion, his family gave Raza money and presents.

## Author's Note

Ramadan is the ninth month in the Muslim calendar. The calendar is based upon the moon, and lunar months are shorter than solar months. Therefore, the actual date varies year to year when compared to the Gregorian calendar. During this month, most able-bodied Muslims fast from sunrise to sunset. We wake up before sunrise and eat a hearty breakfast called Sehri, or *Suhoor,* in Arabic, and then we do not eat or drink till sunset. The evening meal is called Iftar, or *Futur,* and is usually an elaborate feast, often enjoyed with friends and relatives. The menus of both meals vary, depending upon the local culture. This story is based in Pakistan.

Ramadan is a holy month for all Muslims who believe fasting encourages self-control and hunger reminds us to empathize with the poor. Other ways of purifying the body and soul are to quit bad habits, give generously to charities, and meet as a community for additional prayers each night.

Young children, pregnant women, the elderly, and sick are not expected to fast. Around the age of nine or ten, some children begin to keep short fasts in preparation for adulthood. The first complete fast is a special occasion celebrated by the entire family. At the end of the month, when the new moon is sighted, the festival of Eid-ul-Fitr begins. It is a joyous occasion when Muslims wear new clothes, prepare festive dishes, and gather together for a special prayer. Throughout the festival relatives and friends visit each other's homes, embracing and wishing each other *Eid Mubarak.* The greeting means "have a blessed festival." Traditionally, children are given money called *Eidi* when they greet adults. In the United States, many families give presents instead.

Glossary of Terms:

*Sehri* – Also called Suhoor in Arabic, refers to the breakfast eaten in Ramadan.

*Iftar* – Also called Futur in Arabic, is the evening meal when the fast is broken.

*Ramadan* –- Also known as Ramzan in South Asia and Ramazan in Turkey.

*Eid-ul-Fitr* – The holiday that marks the end of Ramadan.

*Azan or Adhan* – Muslim call to prayer.

*Paratha* – A layered flatbread popular in South Asia.

*Lassi* – A yogurt drink, which can be served salty or sweetened with sugar.

*Chai* – Typical South Asian tea is black, served with milk and spices, such as cardamom.

*Chand Raat* – The night of the new moon marks the last fast.

*Jinn* – Beings made of fire, mentioned in the Quran. Singular: Jinni.

Note: There are slight variations in spelling and pronunciation throughout the Muslim world.

# Paratha Recipe

### Ingredients

- 3½ cups whole-grain wheat flour

- 1 teaspoon salt (or to taste)

- 2 tablespoons vegetable oil or melted butter

- 1½ to 2 cups water

- additional oil for frying

# Directions

Sift together flour and salt.

Add a little water at a time, enough to make a soft dough.

Knead the dough a few times, until it is smooth. Let rest for ten minutes.

Meanwhile heat oil in skillet on medium high.

Divide dough into eight balls. Dust with flour, so they do not stick to your hands. With a rolling pin, roll out each to a circle, six inches in diameter.

Brush the surface of each paratha with melted butter or oil. Fold edges to make a square. Roll and repeat the process two more times. For a round shape, gather the edges to make another dough ball.

An adult should fry the paratha on both sides until golden brown. Makes about eight parathas.

Enjoy with yogurt, scrambled eggs, or kebabs.

Note to parents: Children enjoy making parathas in different shapes, and both cooked and uncooked parathas may be frozen.

CPSIA information can be obtained
at www.ICGtesting.com
Printed in the USA
LVHW071140140321
681500LV00003B/75